W9-DGI-539

R0085424901

11/2017

Dear mouse friends,
Welcome to the world of

Geronimo Stilton

THE RODENT'S GAZETTE
EDITORIAL STAFF

Geronimo Stilton
A learned and brainy
mouse; editor of
The Rodent's Gazette

Thea Stilton
Geronimo's sister and
special correspondent at
The Rodent's Gazette

Trap Stilton
An awful joker;
Geronimo's cousin and
owner of the store
Cheap Junk for Less

Benjamin Stilton
A sweet and loving
nine-year-old mouse;
Geronimo's favorite
nephew

Geronimo Stilton

SPECIAL EDITION

CHRISTMAS CATASTROPHE

Scholastic Inc.

New York   Toronto   London   Auckland
Sydney   Mexico City   New Delhi   Hong Kong

ISBN 978-0-545-00902-7

Based on an original idea by Elisabetta Dami.

www.geronimostilton.com

Published by Scholastic Inc., 557 Broadway, New York, NY 10012. SCHOLASTIC and associated logos are trademarks and/or registered trademarks of Scholastic Inc.

Stilton is the name of a famous English cheese. It is a registered trademark of the Stilton Cheese Makers' Association. For more information, go to www.stiltoncheese.com.

Text by Geronimo Stilton
Original title *Ahi ahi ahi, sono nei guai!*
Cover by Cleo Bianca and Vittoria Termini
Illustrations by Silvia Bigolin, Christian Aliprandi, and Davide Turotti
Graphics by Merenguita Gingermouse and Michela Battaglin

Special thanks to Beth Dunfey
Translated by Lidia Morson Tramontozzi

26 25 24 23 22 21   16/0

Printed in the U.S.A.   40
First printing, September 2007

THIS STORY IS TRUE. I GIVE YOU MY WORD!

What you're about to read is true. I, *Geronimo Stilton*, give you my word as a mouse of honor!

Everything you're about to read really happened. I broke every bone in my body — even in my tail! How, you ask? How could such a terrible thing happen to a cautious, careful rodent like myself? Well, if you **REALLY** want to know . . .

Read on!

SNOWFLAKES WERE DRIFTING SOFTLY . . .

It was a beautiful, crisp day in early November. **Snow** had just begun to fall on the streets of New Mouse City. It was the first **Snow** of the year. I love the city after a **Snowfall**, don't you?

As I gazed out my office window, I began to **think**. I was chewing over ideas for my next bestseller. I'm a reporter, which means that I'm drawn to a **STORY** like a cat to a mouse convention. I'm also the publisher and editor in chief of *The Rodent's Gazette*, the most famous newspaper on Mouse Island.

"Hmm, I guess I could write a **love** story . . ." I mumbled aloud. Then I thought better of it. "No, no, no. Too mushy!

2

Geronimo Stilton

Maybe I could write a mystery, something about cops and robbers. . . ."

Then I thought better of *that*, too. "No, no, no. Too scary! Everyone knows what a 'fraidy mouse I am. Maybe I could write about **PHILOSOPHY** — my philosophy of life, that is. *Geronimo: Straight from the Fur. . . .*"

But I decided against it. "No, no, no. Too boring!"

Just then, the door flew open and my nephew Benjamin burst into my office. He was squeaking a mile a minute.

"Uncle Geronimo, it's snowing! Could you take me skiing?"

I smiled. I never can say no to Benjamin. He is my favorite nephew.

"Why, of course, my little cheese niblet!" I said at once. "I'll rent a lodge in the mountains. MY TREAT!"

Suddenly, I heard the buzz of whispers from the hall outside my office.

I opened the door and saw Benjamin's friend Bugsy Wugsy; Pinky Pick, my assistant

"Pssst... pssst... pssst... pssst... pssst... pssst... pssst...

editor; my sister, Thea; my cousin Trap; my favorite auntie, Aunt Sweetfur; my old friend Hercule Poirat, a private eye; my grandfather, William Shortpaws; and finally, my good friend Hyena, who's a total sports nut.

As soon as they saw me, they shouted, **"Since you're treating** . . . we're all coming skiing with you, Geronimo!"

Putrid cheese puffs! This was turning out to be my unlucky day.

HOLEY CHEESE, WHAT A BILL!

The next morning, I rented a nice lodge on **Frozen Fur Peak**. I had to book an enormouse place. When the travel agent pawed me the receipt, my eyes almost popped out of my snout. HOLEY CHEESE, WHAT A BILL!

We headed to the mountain. I had to rent a **HUGE DOUBLE-DECKER** bus. When the clerk at the car rental place pawed me the receipt, my tail twisted into knots. HOLEY CHEESE, WHAT A BILL!

It was late when we finally arrived at Frozen Fur Peak. We immediately headed for dinner at the nearest restaurant. When the waiter pawed me the check at the end of the meal, my fur stood on end. HOLEY CHEESE, WHAT A BILL!

Luckily, I had my AMERIMOUSE EXPRESS GOLD CARD with me.

When we finally got to the lodge, there were so many of us that we were one bedroom short! Two unlucky rodents had to sleep in a small, **dusty** broom closet with sagging bunk beds inside. It was fit for a sewer rat.

We decided to draw straws to see who would have to share this rat's nest of a room. Of course, I drew one of the short straws—and so did my cousin **Trap**.

I WAS IN FOR A ROUGH, ROUGH NIGHT.

As soon as we squeezed into the tiny room, Trap squeaked, "I want the top bunk!"

I was too tired to argue. I nodded wearily, and we both climbed into bed. The top bunk sagged low over my head as Trap tossed and

1. PARKING LOT
2. SUNDECK
3. WOODBURNING STOVE
4. HALL
5. FAMILY ROOM WITH FIREPLACE
6. DINING TABLE
7. KITCHEN
8. PANTRY
9. BATHROOM WITH TUB
10. GRANDFATHER WILLIAM'S BATHROOM
11. GRANDFATHER WILLIAM'S ROOM
12. THEA, BENJAMIN, BUGSY WUGSY, AND PINKY PICK'S ROOM
13. THEA, BENJAMIN, BUGSY WUGSY, AND PINKY PICK'S BATHROOM
14. SAUNA
15. LIBRARY
16. HYENA AND HERCULE POIRAT'S ROOM
17. HYENA AND HERCULE POIRAT'S BATHROOM
18. AUNT SWEETFUR'S ROOM
19. AUNT SWEETFUR'S BATHROOM
20. SKI RACK
21. GERONIMO AND TRAP'S BROOM CLOSET

turned. (My cousin has a bit of a cheese belly.)

Around midnight, Trap woke me up. "Geronimo, I want to sleep on the bottom bunk. I'm afraid of falling out of bed!"

I sighed deeply. Again, it was easier not to argue. I settled into the top bunk and fell into a deep sleep. Until . . .

Around three A.M., Trap woke me up. "Geronimo, I have a tummyache. I want some hot chamomile tea!"

I sighed deeply. This time, I really wanted to argue, but I didn't want to wake the whole lodge. So I got up and made my cousin some hot tea.

Trap fell asleep immediately, but

now I was wide awake! This lodge was spooky, with the mountain wind whistling around it. Slimy Swiss balls! I never should have agreed to go on this crummy vacation!

After tossing and turning for hours, I finally drifted off to sleep again. . . .

But a few minutes later, someone woke me.

"Wake up, you lazy rodent!"

I leaped up so fast, I banged my snout on the ceiling.

It was Grandfather William. "Grandson, why are you still sleeping? The ski slopes are waiting for us!"

I got up, rubbing the top of my head. Holey cheese, what a lump!

OF COURSE!

When I stumbled out of my room, Benjamin planted a tiny kiss on my whiskers. "Uncle, can I ski with you today?"

"Of course, my little cheddar chunk! Just let me take a shower, and we can go."

I stumbled into the bathroom, turned on the shower . . . and yelped. "This water is ice cold!"

Aaaagh!

"OF COURSE!" Trap snorted. "You were the last one up, sleepyhead! Of course, there's no hot water left!"

I tried to dry my frozen fur . . . but there weren't any towels left.

"OF COURSE!" Trap

Sigh . . .

snorted. "You were the last one up, SNOOZY! Of course, there aren't any towels left."

I dried myself off with toilet paper, but little bits of paper got stuck all over my fur! I looked like the Abominable Snowmouse.

I got dressed and dashed downstairs for breakfast . . . but the refrigerator was completely EMPTY!

"OF COURSE!" Trap snorted. "You were the last one up, lazymouse! Of course, there isn't any food left!"

I sighed. At least I'd have fun once we got to the ski slopes.

W-w-what!

THE SOUND OF SNOW CRUNCHING UNDER SKIS!

Gondola

Ski lift

T-bar

After scampering around to gather all our equipment, we piled into the bus and drove to the ski slopes.

We boarded the GONDOLA, climbed onto the ski lift, and then made our way to the T~bar.

To protect myself from the sun, I wore GOGGLES and SUNTAN LOTION. Even though it was very cold, the sun's rays were bright! Especially when they glinted off all that beautiful fresh snow.

As soon as I climbed off the T-bar, I grabbed my SKI POLES and took off down the mountain. Benjamin was at my side. He's an excellent skier!

We began our descent down a gleaming white slope. *What peace!* It was beautiful up here at the top of the mountain. Only the swishing of our skis broke the silence. I loved feeling the wind in my fur. With my whiskers *flapping* in the wind, I shouted, "I love *skiiiiiiiiiiiiiiiing!*"

As soon as we got to the

Long johns

Turtleneck sweater

Ski pants

Ski jacket

Ski mittens

Hat

Ski boots

Ski poles

Goggles

Suntan lotion

Skis

bottom of the mountain, we joined the line to GO BACK UP on the ski lift. But a very rude rat cut in front of us. I heard the mice behind us whispering to one another, "That's *SPEEDY DAREMOUSE*, the terror of the slopes!"

I tapped the rude rat on the shoulder and said politely, "Maybe you haven't noticed, but the line ends back there."

Speedy gave me a look that made my fur

SPEEDY DAREMOUSE

stand on end. He looked like he wanted to grill my cheese. But I stood my ground, and he grumbled and went to the end of the line.

All the rodents around Benjamin and me murmured approvingly, "That's right! He has to get in line like everybody else!"

The pretty rodent next to me gave me a smile that melted the icicles from my whiskers. "Good for you. Speedy Daremouse is a great skier, but he's **awfully rude!**"

21

WATCH OOOOOUT!

The ski lift carried me and Benjamin to the top of the mountain. We were ready for our second trip down. But as soon as we pushed off, I heard someone yelling behind us, **"WATCH OOOOOUT!** Out of my waaaaaaaay! Here I coooooooooome!"

It was that same **reckless**, ill-mannered rat, Speedy Daremouse! Why couldn't he respect the rules of the **slopes**? Did he think he was better than all the other rodents on the mountain? My whiskers were quivering with anger at his behavior!

But just then, Speedy

RULES OF CONDUCT FOR SKIERS

1. RESPECT: Skiers must behave in a way that does not put other skiers in danger.

2. CAUTION: Skiers must adapt their speed and actions according to their ability. Skiers must always stay in control, so they can stop and avoid other rodents.

3. CHOICE OF ROUTE: Skiers coming down the mountain from above other skiers must choose a course that does not endanger those below them. Remember that skiers up ahead have the right of way.

4. PASSING: Skiers may pass on both sides. However, they must always keep a safe distance from other skiers. Skiers should avoid getting too close to the edge of the slope, so that other skiers have room to pass them.

5. CROSSING: Skiers entering or crossing a marked trail, or starting again after stopping, must look up and down the slopes to determine if they can do so without endangering themselves or others. Skiers should not cross in front of other skiers.

6. STOPPING: Unless absolutely necessary, skiers must avoid stopping, especially when it is difficult to see. After a fall, skiers must move clear of the slope as soon as possible.

7. CLIMBING: A skier climbing uphill on skis or on foot must keep to the edge of the slope.

8. SIGNS: Skiers must respect all signs and markings on the slopes.

9. ACCIDENTS: Skiers have a duty to assist those who may have fallen or become injured.

10. IDENTIFICATION: Anyone who is involved in or witness to an accident must exchange names and addresses.

skidded on a stone, lost control, and crashed right into me. Total wipeout! We went flying down the mountain, tail over snout.

Speedy and I rolled down the slope, going faster and faster the farther we tumbled. Soon we'd formed an enormouse SNOWBALL!

An enormouse snowball!!!!!!!!!!!!!!

It grew **larger** and **larger** as we sped down the mountainside. All the rodents in our path screeched in terror and skied out of our way as quickly as possible.

We whizzed past the pretty mouse we had seen earlier at the SKi LiFT. I barely had time to yelp, "Sorry, Miss, I can't stoooooop . . ." before we had already rolled awaaaaaay!

Sorry, Miss!

Heeeelp!

As we approached the bottom of the mountain, I prayed that we'd roll to a gentle stop. But — thundering cat tails! — the SNOWBALL we were trapped inside was headed straight for a huge ROCK! We might not even make it to the bottom, at this rate!

Speedy Daremouse and I both squeaked as loudly as we could: "AAAAAAAAAAAAHHHHHHHH!"

An instant later, we smashed up against the rock!

HEEELP!
I WANT TO GET
OOOOOFF!

I couldn't move. Everything around me had gone white.

I'm not sure how much time passed before the ski patrol arrived with a stretcher.

"Stay calm, now. We'll take you down on

Woo-hoo!

a **toboggan**," the EMT (Emergency Mouse Technician) told me.

I squeaked. "What's a **toboggan**?"

Before I could say "cheddar cheese sticks on a skewer," they had lifted me onto a stretcher. Then they took off downhill at **warp speed**.

"Heeeeeeeeeeeeeelp! I want to get ooooff!" I screamed.

Heeeeeeelp!

I want to get oooooooff!

Coming through!

I had never been so scared in my whole life. Even my whiskers were too terrified to tremble.

My heart was beating out of control.

I couldn't move my paws, but I coiled my tail over my eyes so I wouldn't have to witness my own gruesome end.

How could it have come to this? How could a 'fraidy mouse like me wind up this way? I'd always thought

Thump-Thump!

I would die an old gray mouse, alone in my study with a cup of hot cheddar, surrounded by books. But this was like something out of my worst nightmares!

After what seemed like forever, we stopped. I twitched my tail and cautiously opened one eye.

"We're down in the valley!" I heard the EMTs shout.

And then, before I could say "frozen

cheese pops with chocolate sauce," they hauled me into an ambulance that took off at **SUPERSONIC SPEED**!

"**Heeelp**! I want to get oooooff!" I screamed.

This time, I couldn't even move my tail to cover my eyes. I was completely **frozen** with fear.

After a while, I saw a sign with a strange picture outside the window.

Then I understood. The ambulance had

stopped in front of a tall white building — the hospital!

Before I could say "Swiss stew with chunks of cheddar," they loaded me on top of a gurney that **zoomed** down a long, narrow corridor.

I screamed and screamed, "Heeelp! I want to get oooooff!"

Did I mention that I hate hospitals?

X-RAY FIT
FOR A MOUSE

We finally got to a place called the Radiology Department. A doctor smiled at me.

"Good morning, sir! We're going to take some X-RAYS to see if you have any BROKEN BONES."

Trap, who had been running behind my gurney, snorted. "Oh, Cousin, you always make such a **big deal** over nothing. I'll bet you it's just a little sprain."

The doctor got the X-ray machine ready. Then he turned back to me and said, "Geronimo, you need to stay still."

I nodded. Machines made me nervous! This machine was so big and scary-looking. But I lay very still for a few moments.

X-RAYS are invisible electromagnetic waves that can go through the skin and other soft parts of the body. They stop when they hit hard parts, such as bones, teeth, and certain organs. The waves make it possible to see bone fractures.

I was lucky. X-rays don't hurt at all!

The doctor left the room for about fifteen minutes. When he came back, he squeaked, "Well, well, well, Mr. Stilton, you have every right to complain! You broke every BONE, and I mean *every* bone, in your whole body!"

"I told you so!" I was talking to Trap, of course. Then I fell back onto the gurney. It hurt to even talk!

Trap snatched the X-RAY FILM right out of the doctor's paws. "Hmph. Are you really sure that something is broken? My cousin Gerry is such a whiner, you can't take him seriously. . . ."

The doctor pointed to the X-ray. "These lines indicate bone fractures. Don't worry, Mr. Stilton, we'll operate IMMEDIATELY. We'll fix those bones of yours in no time at all."

I turned as PALE as a graveyard mouse on Halloween.

"Wha-wha-wha-wha-what? Operate! But I – I –" I stammered.

"Ha, ha, ha! Don't be such a 'fraidy mouse, Cousinkins! It's nothing but a *little surgery*!" Trap said.

"Easy for you to say!" I squeaked. "They're operating on *me*, not you!"

RELAX!
IT'S JUST A
LITTLE SURGERY!

The doctor took me to another room to prepare me for surgery. A nice nurse softly whispered, "Good morning. I'm *Corky Carrotmouse*, the head nurse here." She gave me a kind smile. "You have nothing to worry about, Mr. Stilton. Dr. Swiftpaws is a **TOP-NOTCH** surgeon. This is your chart. It has all the important information about your checkup, medicine you need to take . . ."

Nurse Carrotmouse was so nice, I wished I could

Corky Carrotmouse

have stayed there with her! But before I knew it, they took me away on a gurney. I ended up in a room with bright white

lights overhead. An army of doctors and nurses dressed in green surrounded me. They wore masks over their snouts. I could feel the panic spreading through my fur. "HEEELP!"

The head surgeon winked at me. "Don't worry. You're in good paws! **Everything** is under control!"

All the nurses squeaked together, "Everything is under control!"

The anesthesiologist came toward me with a BIG NEEDLE. If I had been able to move a single muscle, I would have cowered in fear. But I couldn't. So I tried to be brave.

The anesthesiologist gave me a warm smile.

Who works in hospitals?

Every department in the hospital has someone in charge. For example, the chief of surgery is responsible for all the doctors who specialize in specific areas of surgery.

When they begin their careers, many doctors take the **Hippocratic Oath** in which they promise to practice their profession ethically. Hippocrates was a Greek doctor who lived more than two thousand years ago. He is considered to be the father of modern medicine.

Doctor

Nurses

Nurses are responsible for the day-to-day treatment and care of their patients. They give injections, dispense medications, and take patients' blood pressure and temperature. Some nurses specialize in specific areas, like children's medicine. The head nurse is responsible for all the nurses in the unit.

Surgeons are doctors who specialize in surgery. They operate on patients to help cure their illnesses and injuries. They work closely with a team of specialized colleagues, like anesthesiologists.

Surgeons operate in operating rooms. The operations can be long and complicated or short and simple.

Surgeons

Anesthesiologists are doctors who put patients to sleep with anesthesia before surgery. Anesthesia comes from the Greek word *anaisthesia*, which means "insensitive." **General anesthesia** makes a patient fall asleep completely, while **local anesthesia** makes only certain parts of the body insensitive to feeling.

Anesthesiologist

There are a lot of other people in the hospital who do not take care of patients, but without them, the hospital would be unable to function. For example, there are cleaning people, cooks, administrative personnel — and lots and lots of others!

"Don't you worry, Mr. Stilton. I'm giving you anesthesia. You'll feel a little pinch, and then you won't feel any pain at all."

He was right! The injection hurt for a second, and then the pain was gone.

"I need you to start counting backward from ten," the anesthesiologist continued. "That way I'll know when you've fallen asleep."

I began to count, "TEN, NINE, EIGHT, SEVEN, SIX, FIVE . . ."

And before I knew it, I was out. COMPLETELY OUT.

While I was unconscious, the surgeons operated on me. I didn't feel a thing!

When I woke up, I was in the recovery room. There was a sheet tucked tightly under my snout. Around me were lots of familiar faces. . . .

WHAT A BIG DEAL OVER NOTHING!

I was completely **bandaged** from the tip of my whiskers to the tip of my tail! I felt like a mummy.

But there was no time to think about that, because all of my *friends and family* had come to see me! They were gathered around my bed, asking questions a mile a minute.

"How are you feeling, little brother?" squeaked Thea.

"We brought a poster that we made just for you!" Benjamin and Bugsy Wugsy cried.

"Can I fix your **pillows**?" whispered Aunt Sweetfur.

Of course, my cousin Trap was jealous of all the attention I was

48

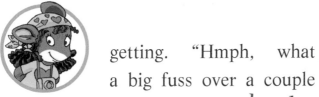

getting. "Hmph, what a big fuss over a couple little bones. Yum, these **chocolates** are delicious!" That's right, he was eating the chocolates my friends had brought me! That mouse had no shame.

"Chocolates?" I whispered, still groggy. "Who brought those?"

Get better soon, Geronimo!

PINKY PICK said happily, "We did, Boss! All of your friends at *The Rodent's Gazette*!"

At that moment, GRANDFATHER WILLIAM threw open the door. "How are you doing, Grandson? When will you be back at work? Tonight? Tomorrow morning? Why don't I bring in your LAPTOP so you can start writing about this little adventure?"

"Grandfather, I can't write," I protested. "I'm all bandaged up! Including my paws!"

Grandfather William snorted. "What a big deal over nothing!"

My friend Petunia Pretty Paws gave me a little smooch on the tip of my snout. "I'm sure you'll feel better soon, G!"

All my friends exclaimed, "We love you, Geronimo!"

Then **Hercule Poirat** even told me a joke to cheer me up.

"Doctor, my leg keeps falling asleep!"
"Don't worry. That's nothing serious."
"That's what you think. My leg snores!"

I laughed so hard it hurt.

Then, one by one, all my friends and relatives said their good-byes and left.

Soon I was all **ALONE** in my room. At first, I was sad, but then I felt my eyelids start to droop. I don't think I'd ever been so tired in my whole life! Before I knew it, I had drifted off to sleep. . . .

A RODENT ALL
DRESSED IN WHITE

The next morning, I woke up with a start. For a moment, I forgot where I was and what had happened to me. Then a rodent all dressed in white came into my room.

She adjusted my covers and said, "My name is **Ursula**. I'll be your nurse for the rest of the day."

She brought me a glass of orange juice. "Drink it down. It has lots of vitamin C. It's good for you!"

"But I can't do anything by

Ursula

First Name: Ursula

Last Name: Smallrat

Who She Is: A nurse assisting Geronimo in the hospital

Her Secret: She can give shots without hurting the patient even a little bit!

Her Hobby: Reading poetry

myself!" I squeaked in protest. "I can't even blow my snout!"

Ursula opened the window, and a ray of sun shone into the room. It reflected off the glass on my bedside table and formed a **rainbow** on the wall.

Ursula smiled. "Don't worry. Everything will be just fine!"

I gave her a little smile back. It was hard to stay grumpy around such a cheerful mouse.

In the afternoon, another

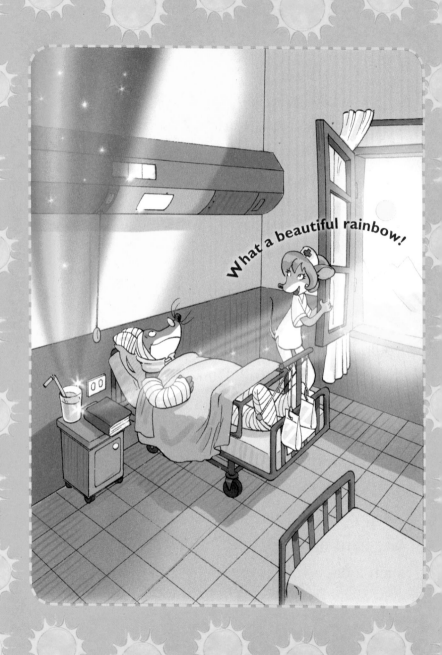

rodent dressed in white came into my room.
She was just as cheerful as Ursula.

"I'm **Mousanna**. Please don't look
so sad, Mr. Stilton. Soon we'll be friends."
She gave me a bright smile. "Now, can I do
anything for you? Do you want your sheets
tucked in?"

I shook my snout.

"How about another pillow?"

I shook my snout again.

"Want the tv on? Do you like listening
to the radio? Care to read a book? Need a
glass of water?"

No, no, no, no.

"How about if I fix you a cheese snack?"

Did someone say cheese? That made me
brighten right up. "Well, actually, I'd love
some cheese!"

Mousanna fixed me one of her special

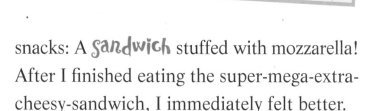

Mousanna

First Name: Mousanna

Last Name: Mousardi

Who She Is: A nurse who helps Geronimo in the hospital

Her Secret: She always smiles at everyone and tells very funny jokes.

Her Hobby: She fixes great snacks!

snacks: A sandwich stuffed with mozzarella! After I finished eating the super-mega-extra-cheesy-sandwich, I immediately felt better.

But I also felt a touch of **SADNESS**. I thought about all the hours and days and weeks I had to spend in the hospital. I missed my office at *The Rodent's Gazette*, and all my friends and family back in New Mouse City. I even missed my cousin Trap!

Mousanna said softly, "Keep your snout up, Geronimo. You'll get better, I promise!"

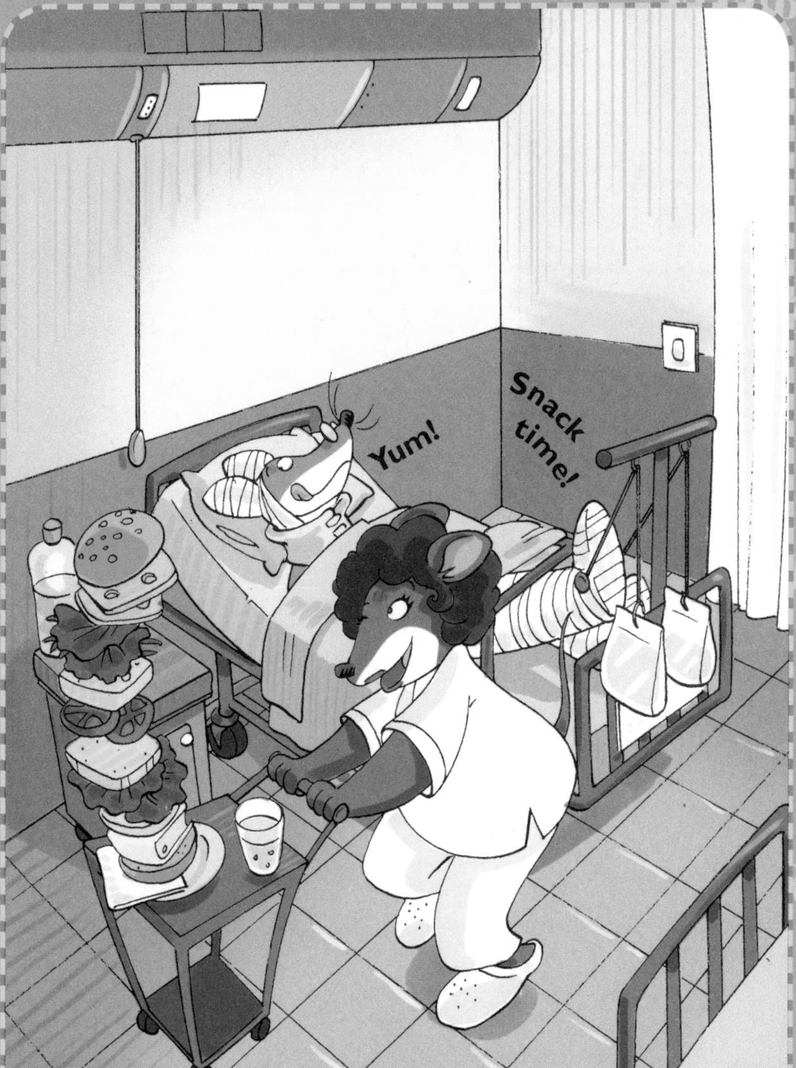
Yum!
Snack time!

She winked at me. "I'm known for my yummy ꜱɴᴀᴄᴋꜱ and silly jokes. So here goes . . ."

She began telling me so many jokes that I laughed until tears ran down my fur. And I found that

LAUGHTER MADE ME FEEL A WHOLE LOT BETTER!

MOZZARELLA CHEESE SANDWICH

Ingredients

- 1 roll
- 2 leaves lettuce (washed)
- 3 slices of tomato (washed)
- 3 slices of mozzarella cheese

1. Ask an adult to cut the roll in half.

2. Place one lettuce leaf on one half of the roll. Add a few slices of tomato and a slice of mozzarella. Alternate adding tomato and mozzarella until you've placed three layers of each on the sandwich.

3. Finish by placing the second lettuce leaf on top of the mozzarella. Put the other half of the roll on the very top of the sandwich. Taste . . . and smile!

HAPPY SNACKING!

How Are You Doing, Buddy?

The next day, Mousanna announced, "I've got great **NEWS**! There aren't any more empty rooms in the hospital, so you'll be sharing your room with two other patients who need surgery. YOU WON'T BE LONELY ANYMORE! AREN'T YOU EXCITED?"

I gulped. Sure, I missed having my friends and family around, but that was different than sharing a room with two strange mice! What if they snored? Or smelled like sour cheese? Or talked nonstop? I was just starting to enjoy the peace and quiet.

"Actually, I think I would prefer having the room to myself . . ." I began.

I didn't get a chance to finish my sentence

before a light-furred rat wearing a **yellow** hat burst into my room. He greeted me enthusiastically. "I'm **Ratty Skimouse**. How are you doing, buddy?"

He talked nonstop. I couldn't have gotten a squeak in edgewise, even if I tried! After an hour, I knew all about Ratty: his *favorite* ski slope, *favorite* food, the names of **EVERY** single friend he'd had since elementary school, and last but not least, why he was in the hospital. He was here to have his appendix removed. He explained

Ratty Skimouse →

that the appendix is an organ near your intestines. Ratty's appendix was inflamed, so the surgeons were going to take it out. He had a tummyache, but that didn't stop him from being chatty!

When my second roommate came in, Ratty greeted him CHEERFULLY. "How are you doing, pal?"

"Good morning," I said to the new mouse, and gave him a warm smile.

But our new roommate did not answer either of us. He climbed into his bed,

Sammy Shyrat

burrowed under the covers, and pulled the sheets over his snout. From the **TAG** on his suitcase, I saw that his name was SAMMY SHYRAT.

When he realized that our new roommate was not going to respond, Ratty turned back to me and started chatting again. He told me that because of his appendix, they had put him on a **DIET**, and he couldn't wait to eat lasagna (with extra cheese, of course). Then he abruptly changed the subject and asked if I knew the joke about COLD-BLOODED CATS.

I chuckled and rolled my eyes. Sammy stayed hidden under the covers, but I could tell he was listening. His whiskers were quivering with laughter!

Why do cats prefer to stay indoors in the winter? Because outside it's doggone cold!

DON'T BE AFRAID!

The next morning, the sun was shining brightly. It looked like a perfect day for skiing. I sighed. I still wasn't sure how much longer I'd be in the hospital.

Mousanna helped me **wash** up while Ratty read the newspaper. After that, the orderly brought our breakfast.

But Sammy still hadn't GOTTEN UP. He didn't seem to want to eat at all. He was hiding under the covers, with the sheets pulled up all the way to the tip of his snout.

"Sammy, aren't you getting up?" Ratty asked him.

But Sammy didn't answer. The sheets began to **shake**, and I knew he was crying.

Ratty went over and tried to comfort him,

but Sammy didn't answer. He pulled the sheets down under his chin as big, wet tears 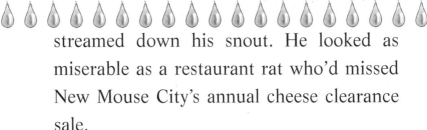 streamed down his snout. He looked as miserable as a restaurant rat who'd missed New Mouse City's annual cheese clearance sale.

"I'm so afraid! This is the first time I've ever been in a hospital," he squeaked quietly.

"The doctors here are wonderful, and the nurses are so *caring*," Ratty reassured him. "You'll see. Everything will be just fine!"

"Why do you need to have an operation?" I asked Sammy.

"I'm going to have my appendix removed," he whispered.

"How about that? I'm going to have my appendix **taken out**, too!" Ratty cried.

Sammy dried his tears and sniffed. "Really?"

"Yes, but I'm not afraid," Ratty said, smiling. "We're so lucky to be in a hospital where there are doctors to help us. Do you have any idea how many rodents there are that are sick and don't have a hospital to go to? If only all mice were as fortunate as we are!"

I was surprised. I'd never have expected a chatty, joke-loving mouse like Ratty to have such an insightful side. It just goes to show that you can't judge a mouse by the color of his fur.

Sammy smiled shyly. "I'm glad to be in the hospital. I know the doctors and nurses will help me get better." Then he sighed deeply. "But I have such a terrible tummyache."

Ratty burst out laughing. "I've got a terrible tummyache, too, because of my appendix. But tomorrow, ZAP! A surgeon will remove my

Many rodents around the world don't live near a hospital.

1   You don't have to be alone in the hospital. Your family and friends can come and keep you company.

2   Don't be afraid of doctors and nurses. They only want you to feel good and get better quickly!

3   In the hospital, there are other patients that you can play with. Making friends will help pass the time more quickly.

4   Bring your favorite toy or game, a good book, or your favorite pajamas — anything that will help you feel more at home.

5   Remember, the hardest part will be over soon. You'll be back home in no time!

appendix, and then it won't hurt a bit! And the same goes for you. We'll scamper around like young mouselets, and we won't have to be on a diet anymore. . . ."

YUM!
YUM!
YUM!

Sammy licked his whiskers. "You're right. I can't wait to eat an **EXTRA-CHEESE PIZZA!**"

DON'T GIVE UP!

With my new friends around, the days passed quickly. We played games and joked together all day long while we all recovered. I was so glad that Ratty and Sammy stayed in the hospital to rest and recover after their surgeries.

One **MORNING**, Dr. Tidymouse came into the room and grinned at me. "Geronimo, now that your bandages are off, you can begin walking again!"

I was very *happy*, but at the same time, I was very **worried**. It had been so long since I'd scampered around on two paws, I was afraid I wouldn't be able to do it right! "Start walking again? Today? Do you really think

I'm up to it?"

"Of course, you are!" Dr. Tidymouse answered at once.

Mousanna winked at me. "You can do it!"

I pulled off the covers and turned toward the edge of my bed. I slowly stretched out my legs. They felt strange and stiff from having been still for so long. After a moment or two, I put my paws on the floor. I was beginning to get excited!

But as soon as I tried to get up, I realized something was wrong. "OH, NO! I'M IN BIG TROUBLE!" I squeaked.

My legs had buckled! My muscles weren't used to moving, and my legs didn't know how to support the weight of my body anymore!

I looked over at Ratty and Sammy. Now I understood how scared Sammy had been before his operation. It was TERRIFYING to think that my muscles would have to learn to walk all over again. I had already learned this once — as a mouselet!

Ratty and Sammy gave me big smiles. "You can do this, Geronimo, I KNOW YOU CAN!" Sammy cheered shyly.

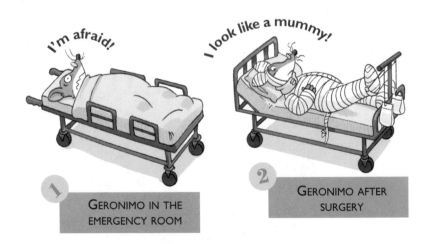

I'm afraid!

I look like a mummy!

1 GERONIMO IN THE EMERGENCY ROOM

2 GERONIMO AFTER SURGERY

Mousanna gave me a walker to help support my weight. At first, I used the walker all the time. Then I moved on to crutches and did a lot of physical therapy. Physical therapy is a special kind of exercise that helps injured mice like me regain the use of their muscles.

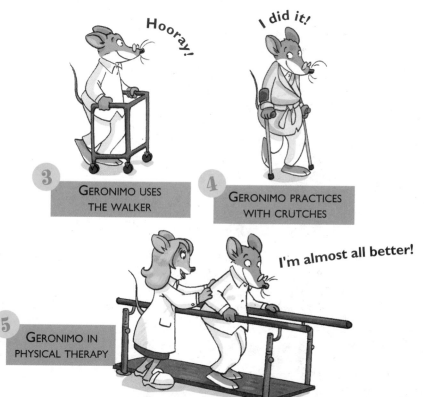

3 GERONIMO USES THE WALKER

4 GERONIMO PRACTICES WITH CRUTCHES

5 GERONIMO IN PHYSICAL THERAPY

AROUND THE HOSPITAL

It wasn't long before Ratty and Sammy were fully recovered and went home. I was sad, but I knew I'd see them again once I was back home in New Mouse City.

I was a little lonely, so I decided to explore the hospital. Now that I could walk, I could go on a tour of the whole place.

Every DEPARTMENT specialized in a **specific** kind of treatment.

Radiologist

I saw the Radiology Department, where X-RAYS are taken to see if you have any broken bones.

Then I went to the

1. RADIOLOGY
2. LAB
3. EMERGENCY ROOM
4. CARDIOLOGY
5. OPERATING ROOM
6. INTERNAL MEDICINE
7. OPHTHALMOLOGY
8. EAR, NOSE, AND THROAT
9. PULMONARY
10. SURGICAL WING
11. GERIATRICS
12. ORTHOPEDICS
13. PEDIATRICS
14. MATERNITY WARD
15. REGISTRATION

Maternity

Pediatrics

Maternity Ward, where babies are born. From there, I went to Pediatrics, where sick mouselets are taken care of. Then I continued on to the Geriatrics Department, where older mice are treated. Right next to it was the Surgical Wing, where patients stay after they have been OPERATED ON. On the floor above was the Pulmonary Department, where rodents with **LUNG**

Geriatrics

Operating Room

diseases are treated.

On the other wing of the hospital was the Ophthalmology Department, where doctors treat patients who have problems with their **VISION**. Next to it was the department for ear, nose, and throat ailments. After that, I went down to the Cardiology Department, where mice suffering from **heart** problems are treated.

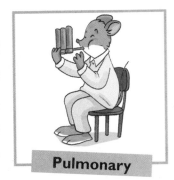
Pulmonary

Opthalmology

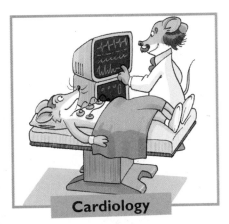
Cardiology

Ear, Nose, and Throat

THERE'S THAT TERRIBLE RODENT!

I was learning so much on my tour of the hospital! As you know, I'm a bit of a 'fraidy mouse. I'd always avoided hospitals in the past. But now that I was in one, I could see what helpful places they were!

I was almost done with my tour when I spotted . . . **HIM!**

It was really **HIM**, Speedy Daremouse, that terrible rodent who crashed into me on the ski slopes! **HE** was the reason I was here!

It looked like **HE** had been pretty hurt.

HE'D had surgery, too.

HE was on crutches, too.

HE was still in the hospital, too.

As soon as I caught sight of that terrible

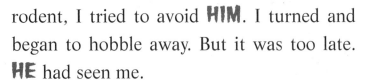

rodent, I tried to avoid **HIM**. I turned and began to hobble away. But it was too late. **HE** had seen me.

"Wait, I want to say that I'm *sorry*," he called. "Since I've been in the hospital, I've had time to think. I realized I've been a real CHEESEBRAIN! My reckless behavior has hurt you — and it's hurt me, too. I am so sorry, Geronimo."

I looked him in the eyes. Speedy Daremouse had been such a rude, obnoxious rodent the last time I had seen him, I wanted to make sure he wasn't making fun of me! But I could tell by the *expression* on his snout that he really was sorry. So I knew I had to forgive him.

I smiled at Speedy. "Give me your paw. Let's forget all about it. And since both of us are in the same hospital, why don't we keep each other company?"

Then I told him a joke, to cheer him up.

We both laughed long and hard as we headed toward the main hall. We didn't know each other very well yet, but we did have one important thing in common . . . many, many, many, many broken bones!

An Experience I Will Never Forget!

The day had finally come for me to go home. I was happier than I'd been in weeks! I was so happy that I leaped out of bed and did a little jig! Then I stopped. I wasn't sure my broken bones were up for dancing yet, no matter how happy they were.

I began to pack up my things and get ready to head home. I couldn't wait to see all my family and friends again!

But before I left, I wanted to thank everyone who'd helped me get better: doctors, technicians, nurses, orderlies — everyone! So I went on a farewell tour of the whole hospital. It felt so familiar to me

now, I could hardly remember how terrified I'd been when I first arrived.

WHEN I GOT HOME, I WAS SO THRILLED.

It was wonderful to be back in my own cozy mouse hole, surrounded by all my favorite things. (Especially my favorite books!)

But I realized there were a lot of things I still couldn't do on my own!

I COULDN'T climb the stairs.

I COULDN'T carry my briefcase.

I COULDN'T drive. (Unfortunately, my sister Thea volunteered for driving duty. She goes way too fast for a 'fraidy mouse like me!)

I needed an awful lot of help from the other mice in my life! I felt terrible about all the TROUBLE I was making for my family.

But my aunt Sweetfur made me feel so much better. "Dearest *nephew*, do you remember when I broke my leg and I had

Aunt Sweetfur broke her leg.

Thea twisted her ankle.

Benjamin had the flu.

to use a wheelchair for an entire month? You helped me!"

Then Thea added, "Do you remember when I twisted my ankle after I fell off my motorcycle? You helped me!"

Next, my little nephew Benjamin hugged me. "Uncle Geronimo, when I had the flu, You helped me!"

I had! And I hardly remembered it. I guess that's because helping the ones you love doesn't feel like work at all.

"Learn to accept help from those who love you,"

Aunt Sweetfur whispered.

I sighed. "I guess you're right. But I still feel bad."

That's when Trap piped up. "Right on, Cousin! I know just how you can make it up to us. Since you completely RUINED our last ski trip with that big spill of yours, you owe us another one!"

I grinned. "You'll all be my guests! In fact . . ." I scratched my snout, thinking hard. "Why don't we go for Christmas?"

Benjamin leaped up. "Really, Uncle Geronimo?" he squeaked.

"Really, my little mouselet," I said. "It'll be a great way to catch up with all my dear friends, since I haven't seen them in a while."

"HOORAY!" shouted Trap. He scampered toward the door. "I have to get home and start packing!"

AT
CHRISTMASTIME . . .

Hooray!

This is fun!

A few weeks later, at **Christmastime**, I kept my promise: We went back to Frozen Fur Peak for another **ski** trip.

I went **iceskating**. . . .

I zoomed downhill on a **sled**. . . .

I even tried riding in a **BOBSLED**!

As for ***downhill skiing***,

Brrrr!

Eeek!

Whoa!

Faster!

well, I wasn't quite sure my bones were up for it yet. Maybe next Christmas. In the meantime, I tried CROSS-COUNTRY SKIING, instead. It was much more my speed.

Finally, it grew dark. It was time to call it a day.

Tired but happy, we crowded in the double-decker bus and headed back toward the lodge.

On our way, we drove past the hospital. I realized that it wasn't all that long ago that I had broken every bone in my body! The doctors and nurses at the hospital had treated me so well that I was perfectly healed.

I stared at the lighted windows of the hospital. They looked like shiny, lonely eyes glowing in the night. Just **THINKING** about all those sick mice, all alone at Christmastime, made me feel very sad. If only there was **something** I could do to cheer them up, the same way Ratty and Sammy had cheered me up when I'd been feeling down. . . .

Then I had an **iDea**!

When we got back to the lodge, I called Thea, Trap, Benjamin, Aunt Sweetfur, my grandfather

William, and the entire Stilton family, plus Hyena, Petunia Pretty Paws, Bugsy Wugsy, Pinky Pick, and Hercule Poirat into the family room.

"Will you come to the hospital with me?" I asked them. "I want to put on a *SHOW* on Christmas Eve! That way, we can *cheer up* all the patients who have to spend Christmas in the hospital!"

My family and friends all looked at one another. And then they shouted, "Of course!!"

And so on **Christmas Eve**, we visited the hospital and played lots and lots of music for the patients. None of us were good enough to go on Benjamin's favorite TV

show, *Mouse Idol*, but the patients didn't seem to mind one bit. They clapped and **sang** along, and some of them even **DANCED**!

Trap made up fun games that everyone could play together. Pinky Pick kept the little mouselets entertained — she always knew the most popular jokes and stories. And Hercule Poirat told us all about some of his most *outrageous* cases.

What about you? Do you have a friend who is sick? Keep his or her spirits up with a phone call, a card, a visit, a little gift, a nice word, a smile, or even a **JOKE**!

Laughter is the best medicine, after all!

Laughter is the best medicine!

JOKES & GAMES

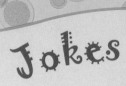

Jokes

THE MOUSE WHO SLEEPS . . . DOESN'T EAT!

Before fixing a cavity, a dentist asks his patient if he wants medicine to put his mouth to sleep.

"Of course!" says the patient. "But be sure to wake it up before dinnertime!"

SNEEZING SWIMMER

Which fish always have a cold?
Ah-choo-vies!

WHAT A SCARE!

A young mouselet comes home from school and finds his father in a fit of hiccups. Only a good scare can make the mouse's hiccups go away.

"Today is your lucky day, Dad," says the mouselet. "I've got something that will make your hiccups disappear right away. My teacher gave me my report card!"

REPORT CARD	
ENGLISH	F
SOCIAL STUDIES	F
MATH	F
SPELLING	F
LUNCH	A
MUSIC	B
GYM	D

A SWEET TOOTH

A dentist comes home from work and says to his wife, "Things aren't going so well at work. There aren't many mice with cavities lately!"

"What are you going to do?" asks his wife.

"I've decided to take on a partner," the dentist explains.

"Another dentist?"

"No — a candy maker!"

ROLLER COASTER RIDE

A chicken goes to the doctor.

"Doctor, I have a problem. I love roller coasters, but after I go on them, I lay scrambled eggs!"

SLEEPY SNORER

"Doctor, I snore so loudly that I wake myself up!" a mouse tells his doctor.

"Have you tried sleeping in another room?" she asks.

A DOG WITH GOOD TASTE

"Doctor! Doctor! A dog bit my arm!" a mouselet shouts.

"Did you put anything on it?" the doctor asks.

The mouselet looks surprised. "No, he liked it the way it was!"

THAT'S THE TOOTH

A young girl comes home from the dentist.

"Does your tooth still hurt?" asks her father.

"I don't know," the girl answers. "The dentist kept it!"

FOR THE BIRDS

A mouse says to her doctor, "Doctor, I always have goose bumps. What can I do?"

"Wait until fall, then go south for the winter!" her doctor says.

DRESS UP YOUR SMILE

A patient says to the dentist, "Doctor, all my teeth are yellow. What do you suggest?"

The dentist examines him and answers, "Well, I suggest you wear a brown tie . . ."

THIRST FOR A CURE

A mouse goes to the doctor. "Doctor, my cold won't go away."

"Did you do what I suggested?" the doctor asks. "Did you have a glass of milk and honey, and a hot bath?"

"I did drink the milk and honey, but I couldn't finish the hot bath. It was too much to drink!"

MYSTERIOUS VOICES

A mouse tells his doctor, "I'm worried. I hear voices, but I don't see anyone speaking!"

The doctor looks worried. "Hmmm, when does this happen?"

"When I talk on the phone!"

Oh, My Aching Feet!

A caterpillar says to his mother, "Mommy, one of my feet hurts."

"Which one, dearest?" asks his mother.

"I don't know. I can only count to ten!"

Friendly Advice

Two mice run into each other on the street.

"I just came from a new doctor," says the first. "You should go there, too. He's really great!"

"Thank you," answers the other mouse. "But I don't need a doctor. I feel fine."

"Look," says the first mouse, "He's so good, I'm sure he'll find something wrong with you!"

Toothless Comb

A mouselet is getting ready to go to the dentist. Before leaving, he puts a broken comb in his pocket. His mother sees it and asks, "Why are you bringing that toothless comb?"

"Well, since I'm going to the dentist, I figured he could fix the comb's teeth, too!"

GAME TIME!!
Look for a Rhyme

What you need: A group of friends

How to play:

The first player says a name of an animal. Within ten seconds, the next player needs to find a word that rhymes with the animal's name. If that word is the name of another animal, he or she wins four points; if it's another noun, three points; if it's an adjective, two points; if it's a verb, one point. If the next player can't think of a word that rhymes, he or she gets zero points. He or she can start the game again by saying the name of another animal. The player with the most points at the end of the game wins!

Invent a Telegram

What you need:
Paper and pencils for every player; a hat

How to play:
On a piece of paper, each player writes

a word. Each player's word must have the same number of letters — for example, seven. Then the players fold their paper, hiding all the words. They mix the slips of paper in a hat. Each player picks a piece of paper. They must then make up a sentence with seven words. Each word must begin with one of the letters in the word on their slip of paper — in order.

For example, if your word is SCHOOLS, your sentence could be:

Some Children Hang Out
On Library Steps.

The Orchestra Conductor

This is a great game to play with a group of friends! Draw straws to see who will get to be the conductor. When the chosen player says "Go!" the player that he or she points to has to sing a song — and get all the words right. After twenty seconds, the conductor says "Go!" to another player, who must interrupt the previous singer by singing a different song. Each player must sing a new song — no repeats. Anyone who makes a mistake is eliminated.

Quick Peek

What you need: A tray or a small table, ten or more objects of various shapes that will fit on the tray, a piece of cloth or a sheet, a piece of paper, and a pencil for every player

How to play:

Place all the objects on the tray without showing them to your friends, then cover them with the cloth. Uncover the objects for two to three seconds, then quickly cover them again. Ask your friends to write down all the objects they saw. The person who remembers the most objects wins.

A Flower for You

What you need: Colored pages of a newspaper or magazine (you can also use construction paper), straws, glue, round pointed scissors, felt-tip pens

What to do:

1. Put two pieces of newspaper on top of each other and cut them into a square.

2. Draw a flower on the square and cut it out.

3. Separate the two flowers and spread some glue on the back of each.

4. Place the top of the straw between the two flowers and press them together.

5. Cut two small circles from the newspaper and glue them in the middle of both sides of the flower. Beautiful!

Check out my holiday adventures!

And don't miss any of my other fabumouse adventures!

Lost Treasure of the Emerald Eye

#2 The Curse of the Cheese Pyramid

#3 Cat and Mouse in a Haunted House

#4 I'm Too Fond of My Fur!

Four Mice Deep in the Jungle

#6 Paws Off, Cheddarface!

#7 Red Pizzas for a Blue Count

#8 Attack of the Bandit Cats

A Fabumouse Vacation for Geronimo

#10 All Because of a Cup of Coffee

#11 It's Halloween, You 'Fraidy Mouse!

#12 Merry Christmas, Geronimo!

#13 The Phantom of the Subway

#14 The Temple of the Ruby of Fire

#15 The Mona Mousa Code

#16 A Cheese-Colored Camper

#17 Watch Your Whiskers, Stilton!

#18 Shipwreck on the Pirate Islands

#19 My Name Is Stilton, Geronimo Stilton

#20 Surf's Up, Geronimo!

#21 The Wild, Wild West

#22 The Secret of Cacklefur Castle

A Christmas Tale

#23 Valentine's Day Disaster

#24 Field Trip to Niagara Falls

#25 The Search for Sunken Treasure

#26 The Mummy with No Name

#27 The Christmas Toy Factory

#28 Wedding Crasher

#29 Down and Out Down Under

#30 The Mouse Island Marathon

#31 The Mysterious Cheese Thief

and coming soon

#32 Valley of the Giant Skeletons

ABOUT THE AUTHOR

Born in New Mouse City, Mouse Island, Geronimo Stilton is Rattus Emeritus of Mousomorphic Literature and of Neo-Ratonic Comparative Philosophy. For the past twenty years, he has been running *The Rodent's Gazette*, New Mouse City's most widely read daily newspaper.

Stilton was awarded the Ratitzer Prize for his scoops on *The Curse of the Cheese Pyramid* and *The Search for Sunken Treasure*. He has also received the Andersen 2000 Prize for Personality of the Year. One of his bestsellers won the 2002 eBook Award for world's best ratlings' electronic book. His works have been published all over the globe.

In his spare time, Mr. Stilton collects antique cheese rinds and plays golf. But what he most enjoys is telling stories to his nephew Benjamin.

THE RODENT'S GAZETTE

1. Main entrance
2. Printing presses (where the books and newspaper are printed)
3. Accounts department
4. Editorial room (where the editors, illustrators, and designers work)
5. Geronimo Stilton's office
6. Storage space for Geronimo's books

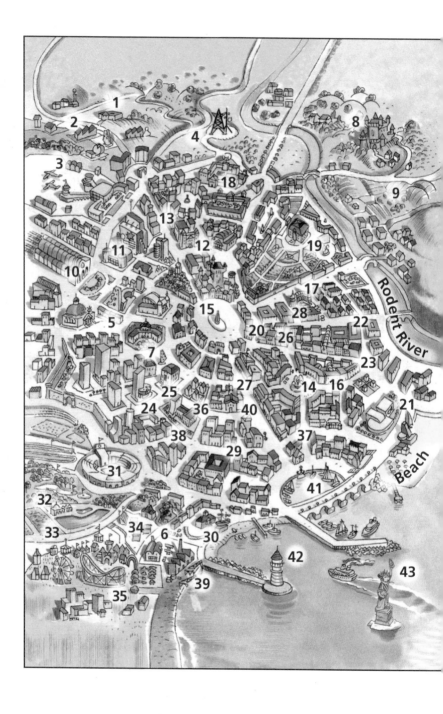

Map of New Mouse City

1. Industrial Zone
2. Cheese Factories
3. Angorat International Airport
4. WRAT Radio and Television Station
5. Cheese Market
6. Fish Market
7. Town Hall
8. Snotnose Castle
9. The Seven Hills of Mouse Island
10. Mouse Central Station
11. Trade Center
12. Movie Theater
13. Gym
14. Catnegie Hall
15. Singing Stone Plaza
16. The Gouda Theater
17. Grand Hotel
18. Mouse General Hospital
19. Botanical Gardens
20. Cheap Junk for Less (Trap's store)
21. Parking Lot
22. Mouseum of Modern Art
23. University and Library
24. *The Daily Rat*
25. *The Rodent's Gazette*
26. Trap's House
27. Fashion District
28. The Mouse House Restaurant
29. Environmental Protection Center
30. Harbor Office
31. Mousidon Square Garden
32. Golf Course
33. Swimming Pool
34. Blushing Meadow Tennis Courts
35. Curlyfur Island Amusement Park
36. Geronimo's House
37. New Mouse City Historic District
38. Public Library
39. Shipyard
40. Thea's House
41. New Mouse Harbor
42. Luna Lighthouse
43. The Statue of Liberty

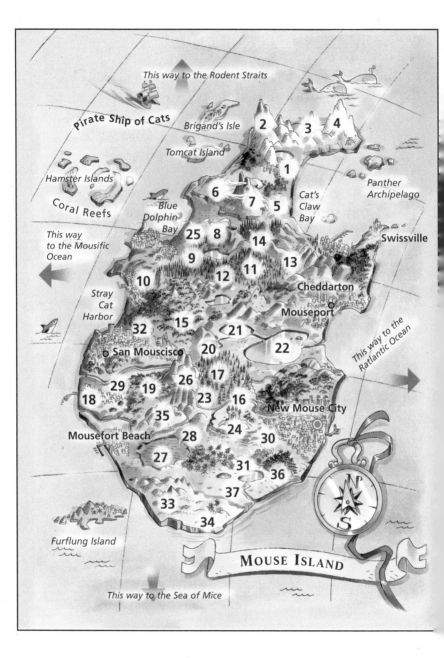

Map of Mouse Island

1. Big Ice Lake
2. Frozen Fur Peak
3. Slipperyslopes Glacier
4. Coldcreeps Peak
5. Ratzikistan
6. Transratania
7. Mount Vamp
8. Roastedrat Volcano
9. Brimstone Lake
10. Poopedcat Pass
11. Stinko Peak
12. Dark Forest
13. Vain Vampires Valley
14. Goose Bumps Gorge
15. The Shadow Line Pass
16. Penny Pincher Castle
17. Nature Reserve Park
18. Las Ratayas Marinas
19. Fossil Forest
20. Lake Lake
21. Lake Lakelake
22. Lake Lakelakelake
23. Cheddar Crag
24. Cannycat Castle
25. Valley of the Giant Sequoia
26. Cheddar Springs
27. Sulfurous Swamp
28. Old Reliable Geyser
29. Vole Vale
30. Ravingrat Ravine
31. Gnat Marshes
32. Munster Highlands
33. Mousehara Desert
34. Oasis of the Sweaty Camel
35. Cabbagehead Hill
36. Rattytrap Jungle
37. Rio Mosquito

Dear mouse friends,
Thanks for reading, and farewell
till the next book.
It'll be another whisker-licking-good
adventure, and that's a promise!

Geronimo Stilton